Investigate

Plants

Sue Barraclough

Heinemann Library
Chicago, Illinois
Peter Hobart Elementary

2008 Heinemann Library
a division of Pearson Inc.
Chicago, Illinois

Customer Service 888-454-2279
Visit our website at www.heinemannraintree.com

Designed by Joanna Hinton-Malivoire Victoria Bevan, and Hart McLeod
Printed in China by Leo Paper Group

12 11 10 09 08
10 9 8 7 6 5 4 3 2 1

The Library of Congress has cataloged the first edition as follows:
Barraclough, Sue.
  Plants / Sue Barraclough.
    p. cm. -- (Investigate)
  Includes bibliographical references and index.
  ISBN 978-1-4329-1397-7 (hc) -- ISBN 978-1-4329-1413-4 (pb) 1. Plants--Juvenile literature. I. Title.
  QK49.B278 2008
  580--dc22
                        2008007264

Acknowledgments
The publishers would like to thank the following for permission to reproduce photographs: ©Alamy pp. 6 (Mark
Bolton Photography), 15 (AGStockUSA, Inc.); ©Corbis p. 9 (Mark Karrass); ©FLPA pp. 19 (Nigel Cattlin), 21 (Duncan
Usher/Foto Natura), 27 (Linda Lewis), 29 (Bjorn Ullhagen); ©Getty Images pp. 7 (Kevin Schafer), 8 Norio Ide/Sebun
Photo), 11 (Tobi Corney), 12 (Sasha Gusov), 18 (Dave King), 20 (Getty Images/National Geographic), 22 (Peter
Cade), 24 (Mel Yates), 28 (Richard Leeney); ©Photolibrary pp. 4 (JTB Photo), 5 (Josh Westrich), 14 (Francois De Heel),
17, 30 (Antony Blake), 23 (Foodfolio Foodfolio), 25 (Frances Andrijich); ©Robert Harding Picture Library Ltd. p. 26
(Alamy); ©Science Photo Library p. 16 (Maxine Adcock).

Cover photograph reproduced with permission of ©Corbis (Craig Tuttle).

Contents

Some words are shown in bold, **like this**. You can find out what they mean by looking in the glossary.

Plants

Plants are living things. Plants have different parts, such as stems and leaves.

leaf

stem

Plants grow everywhere on Earth. They can grow on land and in water. Some plants, such as seaweed, grow in the oceans.

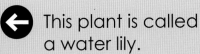 This plant is called a water lily.

There are many different types of plant. Some plants have big, flat leaves. Some have small, spiky leaves. Some plants grow flowers. Some plants grow fruit, such as apples and bananas.

Q

What are the biggest plants?

CLUES

- What plant gives food and **shelter** to birds?
- Where does wood come from?
- What plants lose their leaves in winter?

A

Trees are the biggest plants.

➡ Trees are the largest living things on Earth.

8

All plants need certain things to live and grow.
Most plants do not grow well in cold, icy places.
Most plants do not grow well in rocky or very
hot, dry places.

Plant Needs

Most plants make food using air, water, and sunlight. They need all these things to live. Most plants grow in soil. Soil stores water for plants to use.

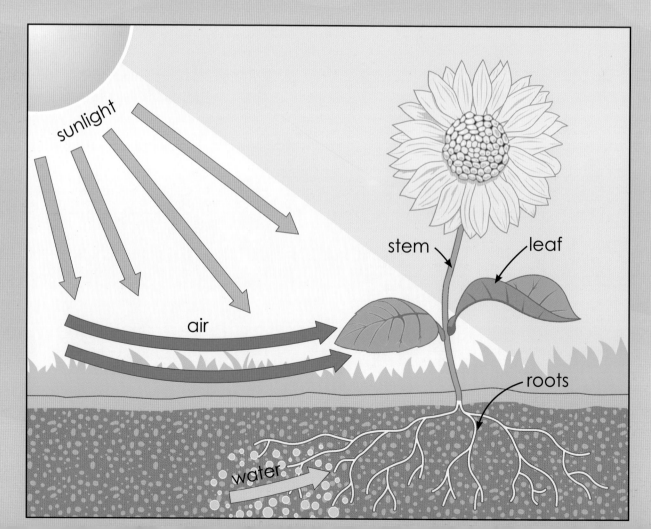

sunlight

air

stem

leaf

roots

water

What happens if plants do not have enough air, sunlight, and water?

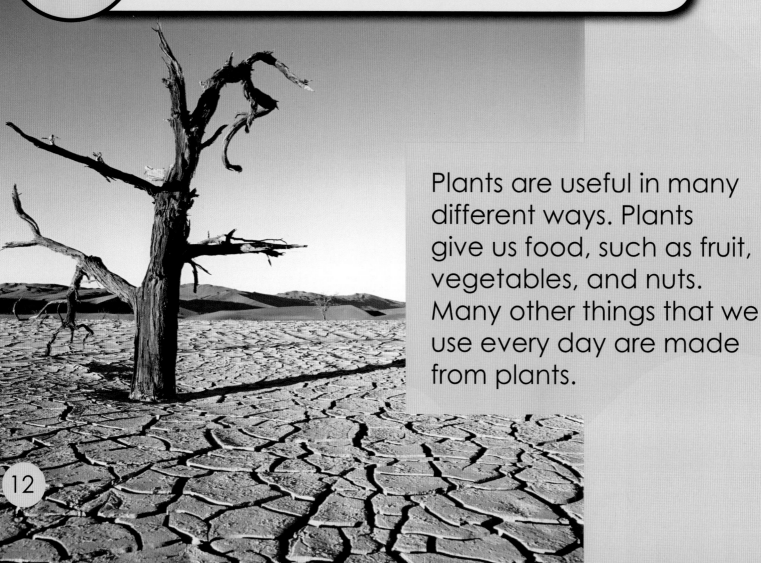

A Plants die if they do not have enough air, sunlight, and water.

Plants are useful in many different ways. Plants give us food, such as fruit, vegetables, and nuts. Many other things that we use every day are made from plants.

Plants need the right amount of water and sunlight to grow well. Plants do not grow well if they have too much water or sun.

Plant group	Amount of light per day (hours)	Average growth in one week (inches)
1	4	1/2
2	6	1 1/2
3	8	2 1/2
4	10	1

Plant Parts

Each part of a plant has a job to do. Leaves make food that the plant needs to grow. Plants have stems. The stem's main job is to carry water and food to the different plant parts. The stem is the part of the plant that grows shoots and leaves. Shoots are the new parts of a plant.

Which plant parts grow under the ground?

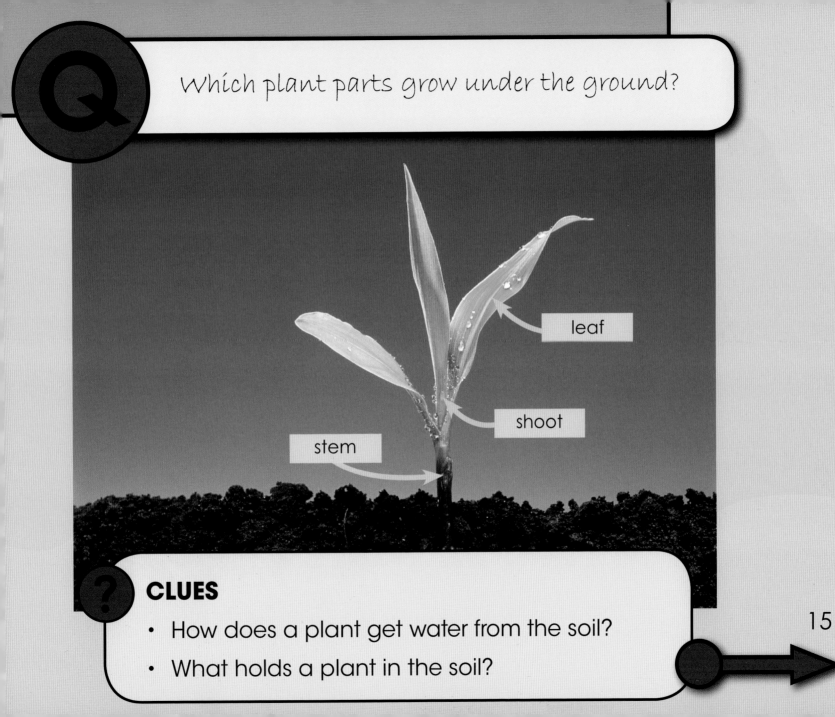

leaf

shoot

stem

CLUES

- How does a plant get water from the soil?
- What holds a plant in the soil?

Plants have roots. A plant's roots pull water from the soil. The water moves up through the stem to the leaves.

This plant has been taken out of its pot so you can see its roots.

The flower is the part of a plant that grows fruits and seeds. The seeds are the parts from which new plants grow.

seed

fruit

flower

Plant Life Cycle

A sunflower is a plant that grows from a seed. Seeds only start to grow when they have all the things they need.

These sunflower seeds will be planted in soil.

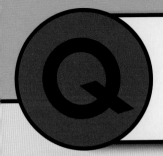

Q What does the sunflower plant need to grow well?

CLUES

- Do plants grow well in cold, dark places?

- What do plants grow in?

A The sunflower needs air, water, sunlight, and soil.

The sunflower grows a strong stem and roots. The stem grows tall and straight. The stem grows leaves and shoots. Then flowers start to grow.

20

The sunflower grows
seeds. Animals such
as birds eat some
of the seeds. The
seeds that are left
fall to the ground.
New sunflower
plants can grow
from the seeds.

21

Using Plants

Many animals climb trees to find fruit and leaves to eat. Other animals eat plants, such as grass.

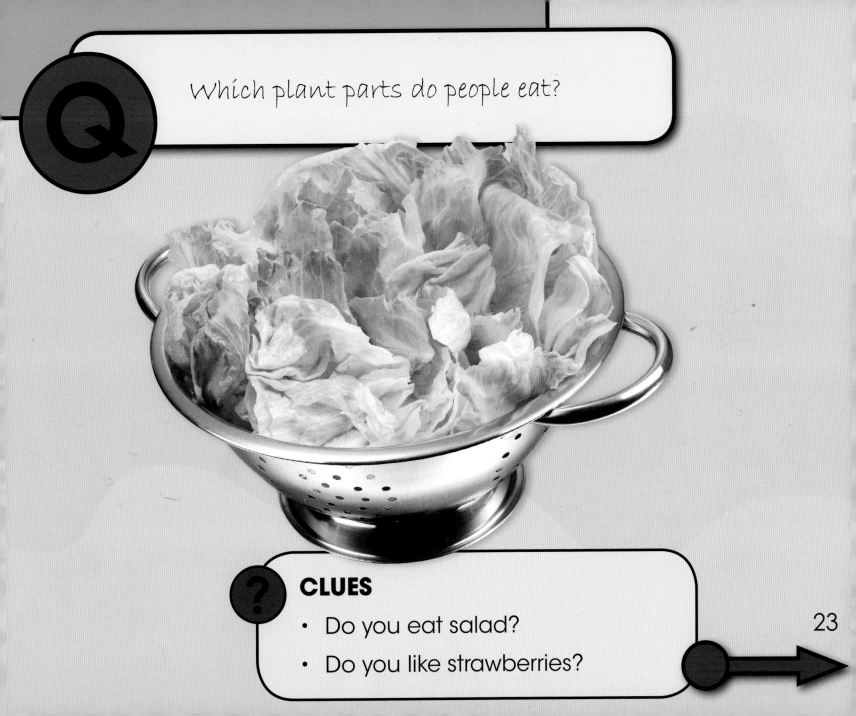

Q Which plant parts do people eat?

CLUES

- Do you eat salad?
- Do you like strawberries?

23

People eat all sorts of plant parts, such as seeds, stems, leaves, roots, and fruit.

Melon is a fruit.

24

People eat many different plant parts. We eat lettuce leaves. Beans are seeds, and rhubarb is a stem. Broccoli is a flower, and carrots are roots.

Plants are food for people and animals. Plant **materials** are also used to make and build things. Plant parts are used as **medicines**. Plant parts that have been in the ground for millions of years are used as **fuels**.

The **sap** from this tree will be used to make rubber.

Plants also use animals. Plants need to spread their seeds to grow in different places. Some animals eat seeds. The seeds pass through their bodies and are carried to a different place.

Squirrels bury seeds for winter food. But if they do not eat them, the seeds can grow into new plants.

27

People and animals need plants. Plants are important as food and as **shelter**. Farmers grow fruit, vegetables, and many other plant foods.

We grow plants, such as wheat, to make bread.

Plants are important for all living things. If there were no plants, there would be no life on Earth.

29

Checklist

Plants need air, water, sunlight, and soil.

The parts of a plant are:

⟹ leaf
⟹ stem
⟹ root
⟹ flower
⟹ fruit
⟹ seed

seed

fruit

flower

Glossary

fuel substance used to make heat or light, usually by being burned. Coal, gas, and oil are fuels.

material something that we use to make other things. Wood is the material used to make furniture.

medicine substance used to treat illness or injury. Usually medicines are liquids or pills.

sap liquid that carries food to the different parts of a plant

shelter something that keeps a person or animal safe from bad weather or danger

Index